750L

LIFE WITH
BLINDNESS

BY ANITA YASUDA

The Child's World®
childsworld.com

Published by The Child's World®
1980 Lookout Drive • Mankato, MN 56003-1705
800-599-READ • www.childsworld.com

Content Consultant: Rosanne K. Silberman, Ed.D., Professor Emerita, Hunter College, CUNY, Programs in Blindness and Visual Impairment and Severe Disabilities including Deaf-Blindness

Photographs ©: Marilyn Nieves/Shutterstock Images, cover, 1; Alila Medical Media/Shutterstock Images, 5; Shutterstock Images, 6, 10; Akimov Igor/Shutterstock Images, 8; Wayne Dsouza/Shutterstock Images, 9; iStockphoto, 13; Hafiz Johari/Shutterstock Images, 14; Sarah A. Miller/Tyler Morning Telegraph/AP Images, 16; David Goldman/AP Images, 18, 20

ISBN 9781503825130
LCCN 2017959677

Printed in the United States of America
PA02375

TABLE OF
CONTENTS

FAST FACTS

- Light rays reflect off an object and pass through the lenses of a person's eyes. The **optic nerve** sends the information as electrical signals to the brain, which produces an image.

- More than 20 million people in the United States live with vision loss. Approximately 1.3 million Americans are **legally blind**.

- Approximately 10 to 15 percent of people who are blind see nothing at all. They are totally blind.

- Some people are born blind. The optic nerve may not have formed as it should, or there may be other damage or lack of development in the person's eyes.

- Brain injuries and diseases such as **glaucoma** can also cause blindness.

- Some people wear glasses when playing sports to protect their eyes and prevent injuries. Regular visits to an eye doctor can help people keep their eyes healthy, too.

- Scientists are working on new cures for blindness. One idea is to use a **bionic** eye. It would use a tiny video camera to send images to the brain.

HOW SIGHT WORKS

Your visual field is the total area that can be seen by both eyes. Your eyes get information from both the left and right visual fields.

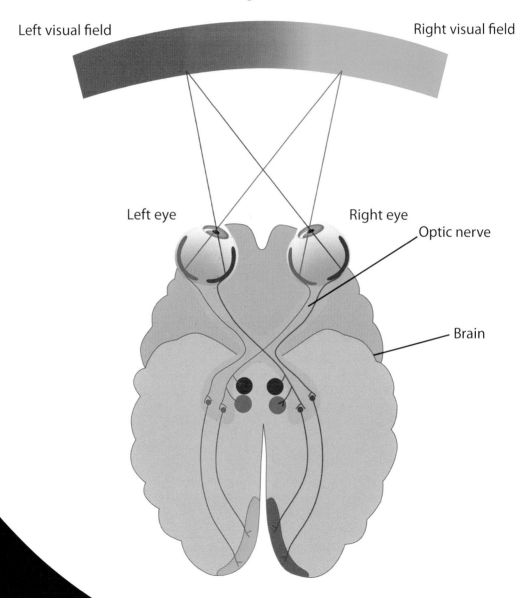

Left visual field

Right visual field

Left eye

Right eye

Optic nerve

Brain

Chapter 1

MIA ON THE MOVE

Mia strode through the subway station. The familiar smell of coffee and warm bagels tickled her nose. She moved her long white cane back and forth in an arc, from left to right. As its white tip tapped the floor, Mia received information about the ground surface below. She quickly stepped to the side when she felt her cane brush against a pole.

When Mia heard the train in the distance, her heart beat faster. She did not want to be late for college again. *Ding-dong*! Mia turned her head toward the sound of the bell. *I am almost at the gates*, she thought. When the sound of the bell seemed closer, she tapped her fare card on the gate and pushed her way through.

◄ **People who are blind often use canes to guide them.**

Mia used her cane to guide her onto an escalator. The sound of the train wheels grew louder as the escalator took her underground and closer to the train tracks. The platform air felt hot and thick on her skin.

▲ Escalators are another obstacle people who are blind often must negotiate to get on a subway.

▲ Raised bumps on train platforms are precautionary measures to warn people who are blind where the edge is.

Mia's cane helped her find the bumpy surface of the ground between the train tracks and the platform. She knew that she had to stand behind the bumps while she waited for her train. As she waited, she heard the conversations of other travelers on their phones.

Then, the platform began to rumble. Hot steam pulled on Mia's clothing. *Whoosh!* The train doors opened. Mia smelled sweat and perfume from the mob of people moving past. She felt people brush against her as they walked by. When their voices faded, Mia stepped onto the train.

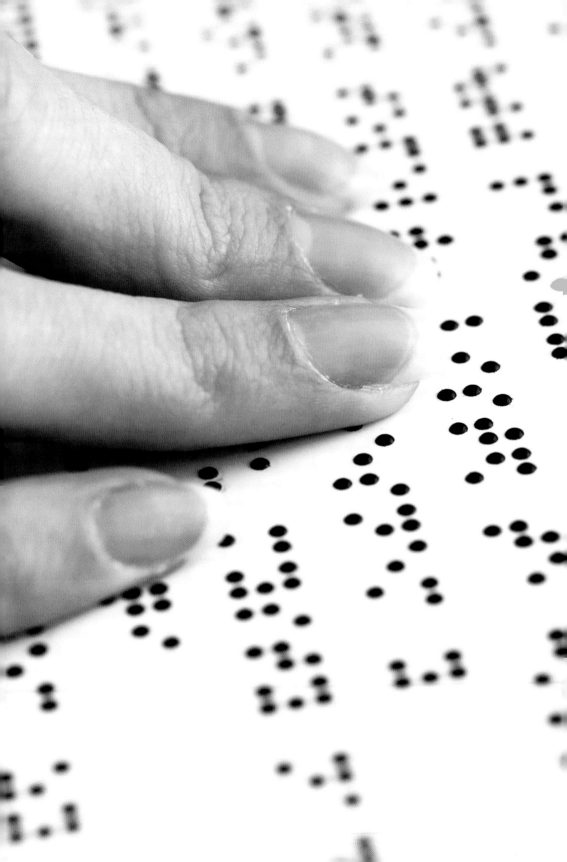

Chapter 2

ALEX'S BRAILLE CHALLENGE

Brrrrrrrrrrring! Alex kicked off his bed sheets and felt for his iPad on the bedside table. A computer voice told him what was on the screen. His fingers zipped to the bottom of the screen. He tapped a finger twice to hear the message.

"Good luck," said a cheerful voice. It was Alex's friend, Jamie.

"See you at the **Braille Challenge**," replied Alex. He told his phone to send his message.

After Alex's dad dropped him off at school, he took a seat in a classroom. There were about ten kids there.

◄ Raised dots in Braille form letters and words that people who are blind can read.

BRAILLE TECH

Louis Braille was born in France in 1809. Due to injury and infection, Braille became blind in both eyes by the age of five. Braille later created a reading and writing code for people who are blind that uses raised dots for letters. The Braille system is used around the world today. There are many new technologies that people who are blind use to access information, such as the BrailleNote Touch. The BrailleNote Touch has a touch surface and screen. A person moves his or her fingers over the glass keyboard to type or read Braille.

Each kid had a visual **impairment**. Some had never had their Braille reading and writing skills tested before. Their chairs squeaked loudly as they fidgeted nervously. But Alex wasn't nervous. He challenged Jamie to a quick arm-wrestling match. Beside them, two girls laughed and chatted about the books they had read over the summer.

The teacher handed out the e-book readers.

▲ Kids who are blind often receive special tutoring to learn how to read Braille.

Alex felt for the cords of the headphones that were plugged into his reader.

"Okay," the teacher announced. "You may begin."

Alex put his headphones in his ears and leaned forward. He paid close attention to the voice over the headphones' speakers so that he could type exactly what he heard into Braille. Similar to a spelling bee, there was no room for mistakes.

Letters in Braille are each formed from a system of six dots called a Braille cell. Each letter has a different arrangement and number of these dots. A Braillewriter has six keys, or one key for each dot in a Braille cell. Alex's fingers flew back and forth over the keys of his Braillewriter, spelling out the words he heard from the headphones. The Braillewriter allowed him to type Braille onto paper. *Click-clack*. Alex grinned as his fingers hit the keys.

When Alex got to the last word, he paused. He couldn't help thinking that this was his last Braille Challenge. Next year, he would be going off to college to study science. He would miss these competitions.

◀ **People who are blind use Braillewriters to type words in Braille.**

Chapter 3

JUAN'S BEEP BALL GAME

The warm sun shone on the day of Juan's **beep ball** game. Juan held his cap in one hand. He smiled as his fingers traced the outline of its brim.

It had been two years since Juan's first game. Back then, the loud *crack* of the bat meeting the ball had made his heart leap in his chest. When it was his turn at bat, Juan had stepped up to the plate. Juan remembered how the pitcher had called out, "Ready, set, go." Juan had listened for the beeping ball and swung. *Beep. Beep. Beep. Thud.* Juan grit his teeth as he heard the ball hit the ground. On his third swing, Juan hit the ball! But he almost forgot to drop the bat.

◀ Beep baseball is a popular sport among people who are blind or visually impaired.

17

Juan held firmly onto his sighted buddy's arm as they ran toward first base. Juan felt his foot hit the base. The base buzzed like a bee. Juan and his buddy made it to second base, and then third. They kept going until they crossed home plate.

After his first game, Juan could not wait to play again. Now, he stood up to bat. He heard his friend cheering him on from the stands. He gripped the bat tightly.

CHARLES FAIRBANKS

In the 1960s, the Colorado School for the Deaf and Blind wanted to create a game for its students. Engineer Charles Fairbanks, who worked for a telephone company, took on the challenge. He looked at ways of using phone parts in a softball. He tried putting a ringer and battery in a ball. When the ringer was turned on, the softball rang like a phone! This invention led to the creation of beep baseball, or "beep ball." Today, beep ball is a popular game played around the world.

◀ Softballs are used in beep ball because they are larger and easier to catch than baseballs.

▲ A beep baseball player listens for a buzzing sound as he nears a base.

He listened for the telltale beeping sound. After hitting the ball, Juan ran so fast that he felt like he was flying. He no longer needed to run with a buddy. He tripped over the soft pylon mounted on first base. But he got right back up.

Someday, Juan thought, *I am going to play in the Beep Baseball World Series.*

THINK ABOUT IT

- Adaptations such as raised bumps on a train platform help people who are blind get around more easily. Think about the places you go each day. Have you noticed other types of adaptations for people who are blind?
- Some people who are blind have never been able to see. How do you think living without sight affects how a person experiences the world?
- Think of your favorite game or sport. How would you adapt it for a person who is blind or visually impaired?

GLOSSARY

beep ball (BEEP BAWL): Beep ball is a type of baseball for people who are blind that uses a beeping ball and buzzing bases. Juan enjoyed playing beep ball with his friends.

bionic (by-ON-ik): Bionic describes a mechanical device that acts like a part of the human body. A bionic eye is a device that would act like a real eye.

Braille Challenge (BRAYL CHAL-inj): The Braille Challenge is a Braille reading and writing competition for people who are blind or visually impaired. Alex enjoyed competing in the Braille Challenge at his school.

glaucoma (glaow-KOH-mah): Glaucoma is a disease that is usually caused by the increased pressure of fluids in the eye. Glaucoma can lead to vision loss or blindness.

impairment (im-PAIR-ment): An impairment is a physical or health-related problem that results in challenges in accessing information or participating in activities without additional supports. Someone with a visual impairment has vision loss.

legally blind (LEE-gull-ee BLYND): Legally blind is a term used to identify people who have significant vision loss, including people who are totally blind as well as others who have some usable vision. More than 1 million people in the United States are legally blind.

optic nerve (OP-tik NURV): The optic nerve is a part of the visual pathway that connects the eyes to the brain. Some injuries damage the optic nerve and may lead to blindness.

TO LEARN MORE

Books

Burk, Rachelle. *Painting in the Dark: Esref Armagan, Blind Artist.* Boston, MA: Tumblehome Learning, 2016.

Frith, Margaret. *Who was Louis Braille?* New York, NY: Grosset & Dunlap, 2014.

Kent, Deborah. *What Is It Like to Be Blind?* Berkeley Heights, NJ: Enslow Elementary, 2012.

Web Sites

Visit our Web site for links about blindness:
childsworld.com/links

Note to Parents, Teachers, and Librarians: We routinely verify our Web links to make sure they are safe and active sites. So encourage your readers to check them out!

SELECTED BIBLIOGRAPHY

"Living with Vision Loss." *American Foundation for the Blind.* American Foundation for the Blind, n.d. Web. 9 Sept. 2017.

Mellor, C. Michael. *Louis Braille: A Touch of Genius.* Boston, MA: National Braille Press, 2006.

Wanczyk, David. *Beep: Inside the Unseen World of Baseball for the Blind.* Athens, OH: Ohio University Press, 2017.

"What Is the National Federation of the Blind?" *National Federation of the Blind.* National Federation of the Blind, n.d. Web. 9 Sept. 2017.

INDEX

ABOUT THE AUTHOR

Anita Yasuda is the author of many books for young readers. She supports Braille literacy for children who are blind or visually impaired. She won the Society of School Librarians International Honor Book Award for science books, grades K-6, in 2012. Anita lives with her family in California.